WORDS THAT CAN'T BE SPOKEN

SALMA ZINEB LAQLALECH

CONTENTS

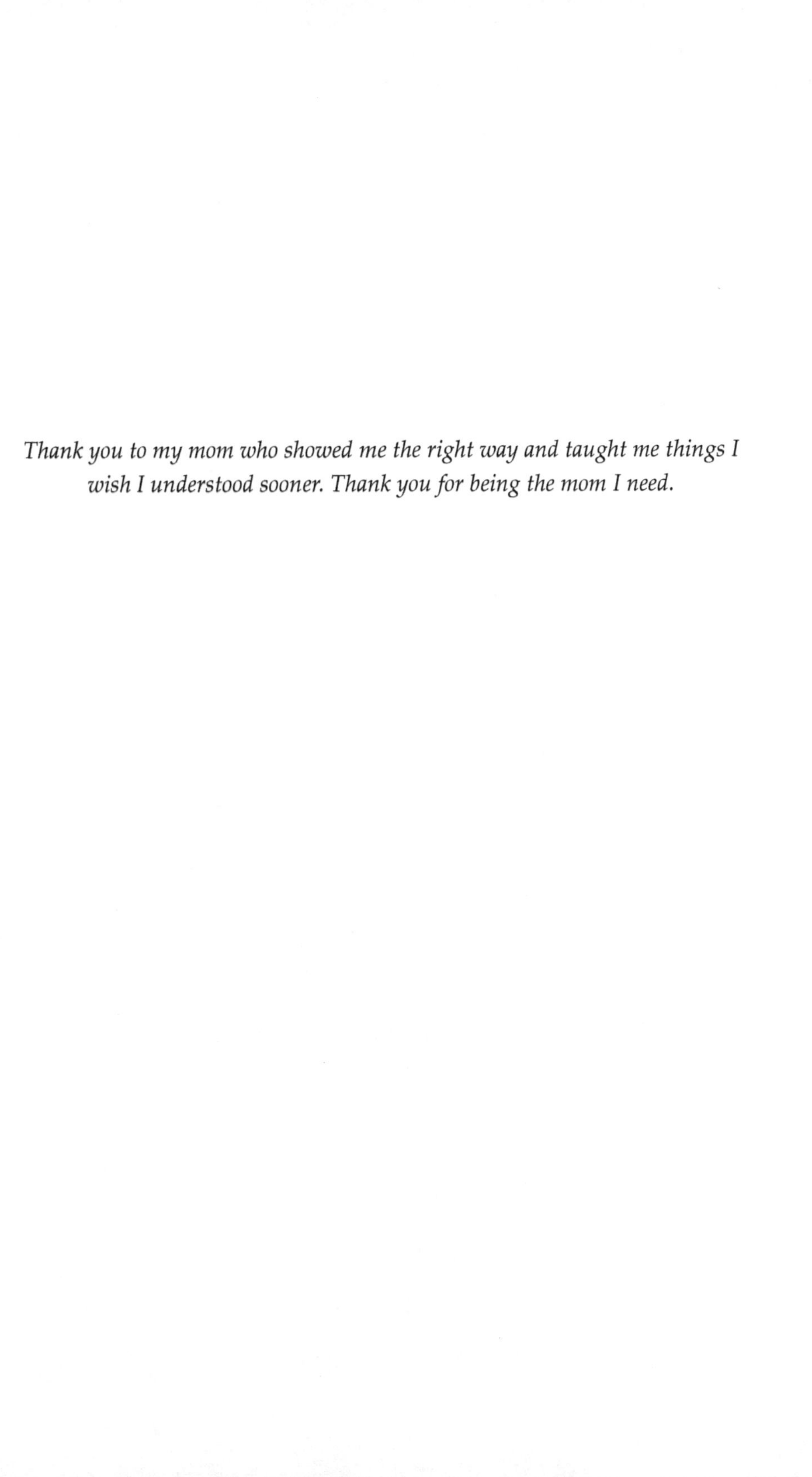

Thank you to my mom who showed me the right way and taught me things I wish I understood sooner. Thank you for being the mom I need.

DEAR READERS

As rose petals fall.
As sunflowers die.
As daisies bloom.

Though you can't stop it, knowing we're the same.
As time passes by.
I may not be here anymore.

My friends and family either.
Or the people reading these poems.

But hoping I won't be forgotten as a flower being thrown in the
*   trash.*
While my writing keeps me alive.
Being passed on.

Like Shakespeare.
But when looking through my future.
I can't find a clue what will happen.

Only longing for my poems to last more than I have.

THE STRING THAT WILL SOON SNAP.

"Oh captain, my captain"
And tho I heard this in a film about poets
This film made me feel close to home.

It may be something that reminds me of me.
For wanting something I have desired.
But when push comes to pull

The string will soon snap and choose what it desires.
(july 6th 2024)

ALWAYS THE POEM NEVER THE POET.

*A*lways the poem never the poet.
When coming close to being remembered.
Or having a familiar smell.

Or having poems being memories in classes.
But will they remember the poet?
The poet that put blood sweat tears into one.

The poet that happens to hope that little girls and boys will listen.
Not by the words but by the poems.
Hoping to tell their stories in them.

To show about the poet.
Not to just show a poem.

To be loved by a poet.
To be hated.

To show kindness in one's heart.

All written down with:
1 pen
1 page
1 soul
(July 16th 2024)

THE MOON

The moon is so beautiful.
It shines when everything is dark.
The stars light up the night sky but the moon shines much
*   higher.*

When everything is going tough just look up to the moon.
Realize to also shine when everything is going dark.
Realize people can be dark but you can outshine them by being
*   better.*

The moon's beauty comes from the sun being behind it.
Showing to keep people close even in the dark.

Even when everything isn't going your way.
(July 7th 2024)

WHY AM I FIGHTING?

Why is it that im always tired
Why do I get enough sleep but im still tired
Is it becuuse im tired of fighting

Tired of trying to fight people to stay with me.
To love me, to care for me, to at least be there when I need them.
But why am I still fighting for them?

Why am I always there when they need me but they're not
*   there when I need them?*
I just need someone with me to support me.

I'm not asking for 10 billion dollars.
They will be my 10 billion dollars.

More than that even.
(July 7th 2024)

TIME GOES BY FAST.

Times go by fast.
I wish I knew that earlier.
I wish I listened to my mom when she told me I wouldn't be
*   young forever.*

And how things will get serious when I hit puberty.
How I won't be a little girl anymore or how people will see me
*   more differently.*
How I can't have anything I want anymore.

That I will have to work to get it.
I wish I could be young again.
Reliving things that I know I can't relive again.

Not caring what people thought about me. Just knowing I
*   was me.*
(august 8th 2024)

PINK

Pink.
The color of love.
The color of beauty.

That's what I love about it.
It gives me so much happiness.
It reminds me of the air flowing across my skin, making me
*   shiver, staring at the pink sky while it melts to the night.*

It reminds me of the love and support from my family.
Pink will always be my favorite color.
From a young age, I've learned to love it then hate it then love
*   it again.*

When people ask why it's my favorite I never had an answer
*   till now.*
(august 11th 2024)

MOMMY'S GIRL

I've always been a mommy's girl.
I'll always be on my mom's side.
I still remember when I was 4 I wouldn't go to sleep till my
    mom would tuck me into bed giving me her warmth and
    comfort.

I remember how I used to wake up in the middle of the night
    and find my mom watching Grey's Anatomy while eating
    raspberry ice cream while working.
When she would see me she would gather me under her
    loving arm.
Let me eat her ice cream even if it would be her last bit.

She's my best friend.
She can be hard but I know she does it for a reason.

She's my mother with all the answers I need from her.
I can be a bad daughter and not follow her rules.
But she always gives me her trust.

I'll never understand why though.

No matter how many times I break it.
She always gave it back.
I love her and I would never change my mom in any other
*   universe.*

I love you, mama.
(august 12th 2024)

WHAT IS MY DREAM?

What is my dream?
My dream is to be something or someone.
No one cares unless you're pretty, well-known, or dead.

But if I die I want something to leave a fingerprint.
Knowing I did my part and kept going.
Knowing that people will hear my name and know me.

I've always had this dream when I was younger.
I want to keep my promises.
I want to get my mom and dad a beautiful house.

One they always dreamed of.
I want to be something my parents will be proud of.
Even if I know they will be proud of me whoever I am.

I want to make history.
(August 12th 2024.)

9

DO THINGS NOBODY THOUGHT YOU COULD DO.

Is it the end of the world for you?
When you are tired of the world and don't want to keep going
anymore.
But you are not realizing you have a purpose to fulfill.

Realizing that if it was the end of the world why hasn't it been
my time?
Why hasn't god taken you already?
But realizing maybe you do have a purpose no matter how old
you are.
You're still here.

Do things nobody thought you could do.
(august 12th 2024)

SUPERHEROES OR VILLAINS

What's so similar between superheroes and villains?
Here's one: they both have the same background.
But they take it in different ways.

When we watch villains we see their backgrounds.
It's full of dark.
Realizing they want revenge and taking all the bad stuff
*   from it.*

But when we look at superheroes, they go through a dark
*   side too.*
No matter what they hold their heads up high.
They take the good in them.

They save people.
Show people the right way.
This shows no matter what, you can be a hero.

You can show the good in you.
You'll have some villains in your way.
Fight, ignore, push them away.

Be a hero.
(august 13th 2024)

SUNRISE

Sunrise.
The sunrise will always be my favorite thing to look at.
Every time I'd look forward to looking at the sunrise.

It's like light came back to life.
Even if I prefer the moon the sunrise will always come.
Chasing away the dark time.

Making colorful pink.
As I gaze at the sunrise as it gives me this feeling.
Like someone came and hugged me and I have the desire to hold
*   on to them.*

It's peaceful.
Sometimes I wish it never stopped.

Sunrise will always be my favorite after the moon.
(August 13, 2024)

WHY IS IT HARD TO EXPRESS FEELINGS.

Why is it hard to express feelings?
Why can't I go up to someone and not be scared to overshare?
Then after doing that, it felt like they would judge me.

Why does the world have to be so judgemental?
Sometimes I wish I never told people stuff.
Cause sooner or later they come and stab you in the back.

I wish that would never happen.
But it did and I keep falling for it.
Realizing that I should keep it to myself.

Not trusting them no matter who the person is.
And as soon as I over-share.
I go home in a stressful pattern.
Realizing I messed up.

Blaming myself for being an idiot.
(august 13th 2024)

13

MY MOM'S SIDE

Mom's side.
I love my family.
I'm not sure who is on my dad's side but I love my mom's side.

They taught me how to be strong.
My uncles showed me what a father figure is.
My cousins showed me to not care what people think about me.

My aunts showed me love and affection.
My grandma showed me patience.
I feel like myself when they're here.

I wish they lived nearby.
I pray that one day we all will live closer.
They support all of us no matter what.

And I'll do the same back.
I learned to be smarter, to love, to care, and to be kind.
They opened my mind with deep heart-to-heart conversation.

I can rely on them anytime.
With their support and love.
I wouldn't change it for the world.

I love my family.
(August 13th, 2024)

WHAT'S SO SPECIAL ABOUT BOOKS?

"What's so special about books?"
I've heard a lot of people in my life ask.
And I'll always say "It's special to me"

But there's a reason.
Books.books.books.
They take me far away from this world.

Something that can distract me from the selfish world.
Takes me to a dream.
A soft dream, sad dreams, happy dreams, mad dreams.

When reading line after line I feel like I'm on a cloud.
When I read I know love stories won't come true in real life.
Knowing reading, makes me feel like I can find someone like
*   that.*

But realizing we live in a generation where it's 1 in a million.
It makes me feel like that's the only thing I need:
To forget and be there.

To love the characters even if they're not real.
That's what's so special about books.

My books.
(August 13th 2024)

EVERYONE IS PERFECT IN THEIR OWN WAY.

Everyone is perfect in their own way.
But nobody sees it.
When you say "Why did God make me this way"

Remember that God is perfect.
He never made a mistake on you.
Everything around you is perfect.

When you put someone down it gets them down.
But remember they're working on themselves.
It's like how you're working on yourself.

Everyone has a gift.
We're all special.
No matter who we are.

We are someone, a person, a human, God's creation.
So thank God for the things he gave you and took away
*   from you.*
He does it for a reason.

Sooner or later you will understand.
And realize no matter what you are perfect.
Everyone gets love from people.
It can be the worst people but they are still special.

Everyone is perfect in their own way.
(August 13, 2024)

THE UNPRINTABLE PLOT

Every book has its plot.
So does life.
Life gives you unprintable plots like a book.

It gives us sad, happy, angry, scared times.
It reminds me of a book.
When there's a plot you never expected.

That's what life is, right: 'never expected'
Anything can happen.
You can be rich and the next day you can be poor.

You can be loved and the next day you can be hated.
Life is full of surprises.
Surprise you never thought it could happen.

The love of your life marrying you.
Or having to deal with heartbreak.
But always remember everything happens for a reason.

So when you look back to books you love, remember how their
    plots go.
It goes from problem to solution.
Problem, solution, problem, and again solution.

Everything is a plot.
(august 13th 2024)

CRY

Cry.
Cry all you want.
No one is going to stop you.

Don't think you're weak when you cry.
Remember you are a human being.
And you have feelings.

Trapping your feelings, making sure you don't show it, will
    only cause you more pain.
Maybe if you let go.
It would make you feel better.

So cry.
Cry all you want.
No matter what, you have so much stuff to take in the world

This is only the start.
More pain will occur.
Over time.

So cry.
(august 13th 2024)

BEAUTIFUL EYES

Brown eyes.
People with brown eyes say it's a 'caca' color.
But when you look closely, you will see more than caca color.

You will see gold.
Warm gold as soon as brown eyes hit the light.
Gold is power.

Brown eyes are like having warm tea with honey.
Having a little green in them.
It's like whiskey.

Maybe blue is the ocean but brown is the dirt.
Brown is the mountains.
And nature.

beautiful eyes.
(august 13th 2024)

WHAT IS A TRUE FRIEND?

What is it like to have a true friend?
A true friend is someone who supports you.
Who shows you the right path?

A friend shows you:
what a true friend is supposed to show you.
Show you to have fun.
Show you that even if you guys fight nothing can change.

No matter how many times you fight.
They keep you close.
When you tell them things knowing they aren't judgemental.

That's a true friend.
(August 13th, 2024)

MY PAIN IN THE ASS BROTHER

My brother.
My brother can be a big pain in the ass.
And he can make me mad to the point that I lash out.

But I know he does that for his 'fun'.
We fight a lot.
And we laugh a lot.

When our mom yelled at us my brother would look at me.
I'll burst out laughing cause he does this face.
This face where he's scared but trying not to laugh.

He's my brother who tries to look out for me even if I don't
  need it.
He tries to go against me.
Or "tries not to go against me."

He's trying to get to know me.
I can tell.
But it's hard to be his friend when he is too annoying.

That is exactly when he laughs when I yell at him.
But I will be his friend sooner or later.
But I love him because he's like that.

He's my brother.
(august 13th 2024)

I WANT TO BE PRETTY.

I want to be pretty.
I want to be the type of pretty where I don't have to care about
*   my looks.*
Where even if I go out in an ugly outfit my face will be pretty.

I wish I could be a blondie with blue eyes.
With a pretty smile.
I wish I could be a model.

I want to be pretty.
(August 13 2024)

22

DO YOU LOVE HIM OR DO YOU LOVE THE IDEA.

Do you love him or do you love the idea of him?
When people ask that I think about it.
Do I love him?

What is love?
Is it a toxic relationship you chose to not get out of?
Is it because you love him or made something up in your head?

Does he love you?
Do you know he loves you?
Or are you telling yourself that?

When you get the tight feeling in your chest when you look
    at him.
Or when you hear him call out your name your heart beats
    faster.
Do you love him? You love him. Love him. Love.

What's the point of love if you can't trust him?
What's the point of love if he hides stuff from you?
Love. Love. Love. Love...

Maybe you are in love with him, not the idea of him.
But how do you know he loves you?
When he says it does he mean it?

Or does he not mean it?
What if he looks at you like you are his world?
Like my dad looks at my mom.

Or how my mom looks at my dad.
Is that how you know they're in love?
Can love be unexpected?

Do I love him or did I love the idea of him?
(august 14th 2024)

23

ALONE.

As much as I like having people around me I also like to be
    alone.
Being alone with only my thoughts and just me.
Just quietness and thinking.

Alone. Alone…
When my mom asks why I'm always alone and says I should
    get out of my room.
I always get mad and want to be alone.

Staying alone is better.
Watching movies, reading, drawing, scrapbooking.
All that alone makes me happy.

I've always been a social butterfly, but being alone just
    helps me.
Helps me get through stuff.
To think stuff through.

Again, and again.

Some people call it depressing.
But I call it stunning.

Alone is all I want to be.
(august 14th 2024)

WOULD IT ALWAYS BE LOOKS OVER PERSONALITY

Would it always be looks over personality?
Will it always be "I only liked her cause she has a nice ass?"
Not "She's beautiful more than anything, my girl,"

Why does it always have to be a world full of boys and none of men?
When you realize that everything you overthought was true.
"I wish she looked like _____"

Why can't you wish she wants you for you and not for your money?
Why can you see she's trying for you?
Will you love her even if she does the same to you back?

I'll take that as a no.
So why do you want someone else?
Why don't you go for someone else?

Why don't you leave her alone?
Find someone you want instead of her.
Stop hurting her.

So would it always be looks over personality?
    (august 14th 2024)

25

OBSESSION

Obsession
What is obsession?
Is it the feeling of wanting more than what you have?

Having the feeling that makes you excited to do it.
Over, over, over, and over again.
Making you obsessed.

Thinking you may have enough but as soon as you let go.
Boom you want it again.
You want it, but as soon as you are sick and tired of it.

You let it go.
Boom the obsession is back.

Back again.
And again.
So is it growing in my chest?

Big and deep.
How do you know?

When you think it's gone but it's there.

How are you so sure you have an obsession?
Does it count when it's something you wish it never was?
So obsessed they say but they don't know the real reason.

Obsession.
(August 15th 2024)

LOST IN MY OWN MIND

Lost in my mind.
Nowhere to go.
Nowhere to hide.

Just my mind.
Why can't I go somewhere else?
Something not so dark.

The endless thinking in my mind.
The horror that keeps going and going again.
Never stopping.

Thinking if everything was fake.
Thinking if everything was not real.
What if I stop thinking?

Maybe if I fall asleep.
Keep falling and falling till it stops.
That's the only way it stops.

I want everything to stop.

To wait.
To at least think something positive.

Maybe if I do.
One time.
Maybe it will change everything.

but im too lost in my own mind
(august 15th 2024)

WHY CANT I HAVE SOMETHING FOR ONCE?

Can't I have something for once?
Can't I have something that I want?
Something I wish for?

Why. why. why. why. why. why.
Why do I have to beg and plead to have something?
Why is it a struggle?

Can't I not work?
Can't I do Disney magic and make it appear?
So why not?

Why can't I have something once?
(august 15th 2024)

OUR LITTLE BUNNIES

Our little cousins.
I hope they grow up stronger and better.
But they remind me of why they do the things they do.

They are annoying to get attention.
As soon as they get the attention they stop.
They are fun most of the time let's be honest.

But they are the cutest little bunnies ever.
I don't want them to grow into a teen because I want them to
  be young forever.
I want them to ask for candy every time they come over.

Ask to watch Disney movies.
And to color.
And to be happy playing in the playground.

They should take the time to be young forever.
Before their life changes.
I hope we will still be close.

Our little bunnies.
(august 26th 2024)

A NEVER-ENDING ROLLER COASTER.

Life is like a never-ending roller coaster.
"It's full of surprises"
I bet you've heard that before and it's true.

No matter what.
No matter how much caution you take.
Or how you try to protect yourself.

Something seems to be off.
Nothing seems good or bad.
An hour before you can be happy, then you are crying in your
*   room shaking.*

It just keeps going.
Knowing one day it will all end.
But I think of life as a roller coaster that never ever ends.

Maybe one day we will know the future.
Like a deja vu kinda thing.
Maybe it will be soon.

Maybe we will never know even tho we have a feeling.
That's the point of life, right?
It's never predictable.

You just keep living.
YOLO
"You only live once."

A roller coaster that never stops.
(sep 2nd 2024)

THE YOUNGEST

Being the youngest isn't easy as everyone thinks.
You have to shadow your oldest sibling no matter what.

When it comes to being not 'the best at everything' you get into
*   trouble.*
The next second you hear "Why are you not like your older
*   sibling." or "Look at older sibling."*
It hurts when you hear that tho.

The next you think you have to be better.
So you do things to make sure they see you.
To get the "I''m so proud of you"

You clean the house to help your mom.
Try your best to be close to your dad.
You study so hard to the point where you have straight A's.

But then it seems to need more.
It seems like they want more.
Or they don't see the hard work I have been putting into it.

*Or when you make one mistake that you haven't made in a
    long time they get mad at you.*

well, im sorry im not like my siblings.
im sorry if im not good enough.
im sorry for being a human.

I wish I were the oldest to feel how it is to be the best.
(sep 2nd 2024)

WHY DO YOU PUSH PEOPLE AWAY?

I know you are going through some things.
Even if you can't explain it.
But don't push people away.

When life gets hard even if you can't explain what's going on,
Stop pushing people away
Or giving them the cold shoulder.

It'll hurt you and them at the same time.
Hold them close even if it's hard.
If they leave you without support

Then there is no friend.
Most likely using you.
But the ones that keep you closest even in the darkest moments
*   of your life*
Are superheroes in your life.

They are loyal to you,
And would rather see you happy than hurt.
So don't push them away.

Let them take some weight off your shoulders.
Even if it's nothing important.
Communicate with them even if it hurts.

Stop pushing people away; let them help you to the light.
(sep 6th 2024)

TAKE A STEP BACK.

Take a step back.
Think about your friends.
Your family.

Put it down and breathe.
Think about how your friends will act when their kids ask
*   about you in photos.*
How will they tell their kids stories about you, wishing you
*   were here telling them instead?*

So put the blade down.
Put the pills down.
Step back from the cliff or the bridge.

Take a break from the world.
Go somewhere people will not know where you are.
Work on yourself.

Then get better.
Then get back to work.
Stay alive.

There are people who look up to you.
Little kids that want to be you not knowing that your life is
*   messed up.*
But remember they think of you as a hero.

And you are one.
For staying alive.
Staying alive from the horrible world.
This dark horrible world.

So stop and think and take a step back.
(sep 6th 2024)

BEING GROUND ISN'T AS BAD AS EVERYONE THINKS.

Maybe being grounded isn't that bad.
It makes me realize I don't need my phone to live life.
I can still talk to friends or hang out with them.

But having a phone is a little depressing.
Sure people can think what I'm saying is wrong but I have a
reason.
Once upon a time there was a girl, let's call her Lily.

She did everything to keep her phone on her no matter what she
needed her phone.
Once her mom took her phone.
She turned depressed.

sad, broken.
She thought life wouldn't get worse.
But then she realizes there's more to life.

She realized her life was better than behind screens.
So she redid her whole room even.
She read more and more.

She got out and saw the world more.
She went to places you would see on the internet.
She was more alive.

That Lily was me.
My mom wanted to give me my phone back.
But I kept saying no.

I felt good to look at the world in a different way.
(sep 7th 2024)

WHY DO PEOPLE CHEAT?

Why do people cheat?
It's either they don't love the person they are with,
Or they do it for fun and break other people's hearts.

But why *is the real question?*
If you love someone else why be with another person?
Why aren't you with the person you love?

Why do you have to break someone else's heart?
Knowing that your heart is also broken.
If you want another girl or guy go get her/him.

Why do people have to cheat knowing they are hurting other
*   people?*
(sep 9th 2024)

WHY ARE YOU SO RUDE?

It hurts when someone is being rude to you for no reason.
It hurts to the point you're wondering if you're in the wrong.
Sure some have an RBF.

But talking about when you're not doing anything wrong and
*   they just start being mean.*
It's like making you feel like you did something.
Like existing is a problem.

Or when they're mad they want everyone to be mad.
I don't like that. As a matter of fact I hate that.
I hate it so much cause it makes me become pitful.

I go and lock my room and think I'm the problem.
Like what I'm saying is a problem.
But I don't know what to do.

I'm stuck in the middle.
Crying and confusion are too much in my mind.
I hate when people are rude.

For fun yes.
Like joking around I get it.
But like doing it when it's serious I can't deal with it.

I hate it so much how sensitive I am but it's the honest truth.
No matter who you are.
A father, a husband, a best friend, a friend, a cousin, an uncle,
    an aunt, a mother, a son, a brother, a sister.

It hurts.
So please stop being disrespectful or rude or life is already those
    things.
Cause it's not.

I know a lot of people get hurt and it's not fair.
(sep 11th 2024)

John wayne

If I had to be a character it would be John Wayne.
Because he is either facing the world or chasing a person.
Because of love.

No matter who you are I'm always going to help.
As soon as you come into my life.
You're stuck.

And I may be crazy.
But I'm always facing everything in the world.
Or chasing people to stay with me.

And getting hurt more than I should.
But it happens.
It hurts.

To be a lover you have to be a fighter.
I fought for the people I adore.

So if I were a character it would be John Wayne.
(Sep 11 2024)

IM A STICK FIGURE.

If people looked into me more they would realize im empty.
Im the brightest star.
But the most distant.

I don't know why.
but I can fake my emotions
But sometimes im empty.

Im not sure how to fill it in.
What is missing?
What is it?

Why can't I know?
Why do I fake it with emotions?
So people don't realize it.

I talk a lot.
Im loud.
Im sad.

Im mean.
Im annoying.
Im too much.

But why can't you realize im as empty as a stick figure?
(Sep 16 2024)

HELPLESS

Helpless.
I'm helpless.
So helpless.

I feel like people can knock me down any time.
I feel like I'm too easy.
I need to put a huge brick wall on.

I need to protect myself.
How?
That's the real question.
How?

I feel like something inside me is dying.
I feel like there is something abandoned.
Something I had is gone.

I guess there's no more excitement in the world.
The world is dull.
Hurtful.

Horrible.
Disgusted.

Unless I do something but I'm helpless with nothing.
(Sep 16, 2024)

38

THE BEST TIME OF THE YEAR.

Winter is coming.
The comfort air.
The world is more peaceful.

Taking pleasure in the world.
This is the one time the world seemed so sweet.
Charming trees.

Lights lighting up downtown.
People drinking hot cocoa.
People having fun.

Ice skating with your friends.
Watching holiday movies with family.
Going around the neighborhoods to see the lights or rate
    houses.

Baking delightful cookies.
Winter is here.

That means the world is much sweeter.
(sep 16 2024)

DROWNING IN YOUR OWN MEMORY.

Do you know that feeling in your chest,
The feeling when you look back in a memory.

But when looking back.
Wishing and wishing you can relive your childhood.
But you can't.

That feeling in my chest.
It's something that aches.
That wrecks.
Like a boat.
In the middle of the ocean while a storm breaks lose.

And when drowning in your own memories,
Wondering how deep can you go.
While making new ones with the people you love.

We never know how deep our memories can go.

But they will always keep going.
(nov 24th 2024)

WHATS THE DIFFERENCES BETWEENS A MOTHER AND A FATHER?

"Wow, he cleans the dishes he's going to be a great husband."
"She's going to be a mother she has to learn to clean the
dishes."
Do you see the difference.

Do you see how mean it is.
Why can't it be
"He's a father/ husband that's what he's got to do"?

Just because he's helping
he's the best husband in the world.
If a mother brought pizza for her kids she's the worst mother.
But if the father brought pizza for his kids he's a "cool dad".

Is it cause he's a boy?
Let's remember that single moms need more respect for
working and supporting.
Some moms out there have to do everything for their kids cause
their so-called husbands can't do it.

The point for a husband is to support and provide whatever he
can. Just because he works doesn't give him an excuse.
Sure he works; so does the wife.
So it doesn't matter.

A father and husband are supposed to help around sure that's a
good husband but just because a wife is a girl doesn't make
her any different.
(sep 29 2024)

41

PEOPLE ARE FLIES.

Think of people as a fly that you can't seem to catch.
See, no matter how old you are, there will be people in the way.
You can be famous and there is something in the way.

But what you need to do is push them out.
Push what they say about you.
Cause you have to know Yourself.

Not what Flies calls you.
Or what they say about you.
You just got to know you.

So having a fly buzzing in your ear you got to smush it.
And throw it away.

Don't think you can't do something cause flies say you can't;
*   because you can.*
(oct 7th 2024)

WE WRITE SO PEOPLE CAN UNDERSTAND.

*"We want to be seen and heard, but it's hard when people don't
    understand"*
*And though I heard someone say to me while writing "Words
    That Can't Be Spoken"*
I understand.

The word is judgment.
You can't overshare.
That you must keep things to yourself.

And when suffering in silence hurts as bad as getting stabbed.
*Just know there are people out there going through the same
    thing.*

We write so people can listen.
Will they read so they can understand?
(dec 1st 2024)

43

SOMEONE'S FIRST CHOICE.

Gold rims, golden life.
Waiting for something golden to happen.
Waiting to be someone's first choice.

They can think about me first before anyone else when someone
*   is asking.*
To know right away that they want me no matter what
*   happens.*
That they would stand by me.

To be by my side when no one can.
Someone that can be my water when stuck in a dry desert.

When golden life comes, it's the person who's gold that shines.
(oct 12th 2024)

WE ARE SIMILAR TO PLANETS BEING SHOWN IN THE NIGHT SKY.

Planets are being shown in the night sky.
Trying to be noticed by the people on earth.
Even if the people think it's a star.

But when looking through a telescope.
Finding the beauty in Saturn and the dust of its rings.
Or Venus the hottest planet blazing through the night sky.

Maybe we are the same as plantes.
Trying to get people's attention
To show we are something bright.

To show if they looked a little closer.
They wouldn't just see light shining in the night sky.
They would be more delightful knowing it's not just stars.

The brightest planets that shine in the night air are the most
  distant.
(oct 12th 2024)

45

WE CAN'T CHOOSE OUR PARENTS BUT CAN PICK WHO WE ARE.

We can't choose our parents.
but we can choose who we are.

When you blame your parents for something you did.
But remember that You did.
You or yourself can change over time.

But blaming the parents isn't the right way.
By knowing the right and wrong.
Knowing making mistakes is ok and we can avoid them in the
*   future.*

Just make sure you know the path you're going and let god
*   guide the others.*
(oct 12th 2024)

I DON'T WANT TO BE A FORGOTTEN FLOWER.

A flower that is forgotten to be watered.
A rose that starts to bloom.
So what can I be?

Can I be forgotten, a flower that hasn't been watered?
Thrown in the trash.
Forgotten.

No.No.No.No.
That is not it.
I don't want to be forgotten.

I want to be remembered.
Like a rose.
Wait no.

I want to be a sunflower.
That gets the attention from the hot warm sun.
Shinning bright.

Sure a rose is pretty.
But sunflowers stand stronger.

I would rather be a sunflower who's never forgotten from
    the sun.
(oct 12th 2024)

47

IM THE WRITER BUT NOT THE WORDS.

I may be a writer.
But I'm not the words.
Tho I write differently than the way I talk.

But it's the words that come through my heart.
And I shall let the words flow.
Like the fall of the river.

I write the words.
But I'm not the words themselves.
Each word I write comes from a different insight.

My mind and heart take 2 different versions of life.
But one will write while the other helps.

I write the words.
But I'll never be the words.
(dec 8th 2024)

ALL PRETTY TOGETHER EVEN IF SOMETHING IS HIDDEN THAT'S HURTING.

River, moon.
Sea, sky.
All so related.

They all reflect on each other.
If one falls apart it's not as pretty anymore.
It reminds me of a family.

One falls apart.
The others take a part.
Why stay with someone who hurts you?

River, moon, sea, sky: they are all pretty together but there is
*   something hidden in them that's hurting.*
(oct 18th 2024)

LEAVE ME ALONE.

"Leave me alone!"
Something I wish I could say.
If it wasn't disrespectful I would.

Why can't I be alone?
To lock myself in a cave of my imagination.
To be in a fairytale and wait for my "prince"

But there's not one "prince"
All I have to do is fight for myself.

All I want is to be alone.
(oct 18th 2024)

MUSIC

Music.
Music takes a different part of my soul.
Putting on headphones.

Listening to the word.
And not just the world.
And the mean comments.

Being in a different world.
Sure, books do the same.
But music...

Music is something different.
The peace and quiet...
Something warm fills my soul.

Music...
(oct 19 2024)

THE LIBRARY IN MY MIND.

If I had a book in every lesson I learned
I have a library
As I grow older, there will be more books added

But these lessons will never be forgotten
As they imprinted in my mind
As I stand in the library of my mind

I can't decide which one is the best lesson
When the lesson helped with the future

As the books continue
(dec - 8th -2024)

WORDS THAT CAN'T BE SPOKEN.

Words that can't be spoken.
Most of the time.
When writing them down helps.

So people understand.
All people want to be heard, to be seen.
If people saw what war is in your mind,

Oh how easy it would be for them to understand...
But they don't.
So you put on a smile.
And walk around.

While a hurricane is happening
In your mind.

Words that can't be spoken...
(oct 26th 2024)

DON'T LET THEM STOP YOU FROM LIVING YOUR LIFE.

People won't like what you do.
But you do it anyway.
No matter what.

People are going to hate.
Hate has 4 letters.
So does love.

Just because people hate what you do.
Or dislike it.
Do it for you.

Don't let them stop you from living your dream.
(nov 9th 2024)

TAKE MY HAND.

Writing, writing, writing.
Wish that people could understand why I love it.

reaching out and helping people understand that they're not
    alone.
That's what I'll do.
Hoping people can see that it's not only them that go through
    things.

That one thing can change your life for the better good.
So showing people that I can understand.
That knowing you can feel the same way.

And saving people from doing something that can end them in
    the beginning.
By telling them they are not alone.
That there are;

Hundreds
Thousands
Millions

Billions

Of people going through the same thing.

Take my hand.
and reach.
Wishing I can pull you out.

To pull you out from an ocean of your broken heart.
(nov 19th 2024)

LIFE IS A TEST.

Life is to be tested.
To see if you can handle the problems.
To see even if you are trying to run away.

It will always come back.
R.U.N.N.I.N.G
A.W.A.Y

Something so easy.
But so quick to come back.
It's like its own little karma.

It's always 2 steps ahead.
2 steps while you get to 1.

It's like you are stuck in a dead end of a cliff and the only way
    to get out is to jump.
But at the same time.
time…
Time goes too fast.

We can't catch it—every time we do.
Snap.
It's done.

So here we are, being tested over and over again it'll the time
    runs out.
(nov 19th 2024.

I WILL BE SOMETHING.

I used to be told that I "wouldn't be anything in life."
But now when I think about it.
I will be something.

It's not a want.
It's a will.
Something that will happen.

And I pray to god it will prove people wrong.
If I am happy with what I do.

Then that's something.
(nov 6th 2024)

BE THE BEST VISION OF YOUR SELF IN YOUR MIND.

People see different versions of your self.
In other people's eyes you are:

Quiet.
Hard to open up.
Annoying.
Kind.
Joyful.
Too loud.

But what version are you?
What do you see in your self?
Other people may see you differently then how you see your
*   self.*

But be the best vision of your self in your mind.
(nov 18th 2024)

THE FEELING IN MY CHEST.

"Are you ok?"
Something I get asked.
I'll always say "yes."

But if they wanted it on a deeper level.
I would say I don't know.
I'm not sure if I'm:
Happy, sad, angry, annoyed.

Or anything of that matter.
I can sound depressing.
But what can a girl do?

I don't know how to explain.
The feeling in my chest.

(nov 19 2024)

PLAYLIST ♪♪

- *Lonesome town by Ricky nelson.*
- *Telephones by Vacations*
- *not a lot, just Forever by Adrianne Lenker*
- *I know it's over - 2011 remaster by The Smiths*
- *Je te laisserai des mots by patrick watson.*
- *Flash by Cigarettes After Sex.*
- *I'm a Firefighter By Cigarettes After Sex*
- *Opera House By Cigarettes after sex.*
- *For the First Time by Mac DeMarco*
- *John Wayne by Cigarettes After Sex.*
- *Cry by Cigarettes After Sex.*
- *(dream) by Salvia Palth*
- *Heart to heart by Mac DeMarco*
- *Touch by Cigarettes After Sex*
- *Velvet Ring by Big Thief*
- *Watching Him Fade Away by Mac DeMarco*
- *Moonlight on the River by Mac DeMarco*
- *Scott Street by Phoebe Bridgers*
- *Fade Into You by Mazzy Star*
- *Where'd All the Time Go? By Dr.Dog*
- *Here With Me by d4vd*

- *I Love You So by The Walters*
- *i love you by Billie Eilish*
- *my future by Billie Eilish*
- *Truly by Cigarettes After Sex*
- *The Cut That Always Bleeds by Conan Gray.*
- *Happiness is a butterfly by Lana Del Rey*
- *Anything by Adrianne Lenker*
- *These Days by Nico*
- *Moon River by Frank Ocean.*
- *Chamber Of Reflection by Mac DeMarco*
- *Space Song by Beach House*
- *i was all over her by Salvia Palth*
- *I Want the One I Can't Have - 2011 remaster by The Smiths*
- *Only One Who Know by Arctic Monkeys.*
- *House Song by Searows*
- *Strange by Celeste*
- *Change by Alex G*
- *Fear by Current Joys*
- *What Would I Do? By Strawberry Guy*
- *Blondie by Current Joy*
- *welcome and goodbye by Dream, Ivory.*

https://open.spotify.com/playlist/01osCulKxxcWlisYd7p Nm4?si=81638f47db854ddb